COOLIES

by Yin · illustrated by Chris Soentpiet

PHILOMEL BOOKS

Every year PawPaw—my grandmother—prepares a special feast of tofu, mushrooms, vegetables, and winter melon soup in honor of the Ching Ming Festival. On this occasion, we crouch on our knees and kowtow with the burning incense in our hands before we eat.

"Why are we bowing to a bowl of oranges?" I ask one year.

PawPaw laughs. "We're not bowing to the fruits. This is how we show respect and honor our ancestors."

"Our ancestors?" I say.

"Yes, your ancestors!" she says. "Let me tell you of two we do not forget. Of my *bok-gong*—my great-grandfather—and his brother."

A long, long time ago in China—in the mid-1800s—there was a rebellion against the government by the people. Our poor country! Thousands died of hunger because the crops weren't planted or harvested. Thousands could not find work. Your great-great-great-grandfather Shek was among them.

News of laborers needed in America quickly spread throughout the village of Canton. Desperate for work, the family decided that Shek and his little brother Wong should go to this new land. They would have to leave their little brothers and mother behind in China.

"Ma, don't worry," Shek reassured her as he packed. "I will send money home and our family will starve no more. And I will take care of Little Wong, I promise."

The two brothers bowed good-bye to their family and boarded the overcrowded ship with hundreds of others frantic for work.

The motion of the ship made many sea-sick—especially Little Wong. Eventually he got used to the movement of the ocean waves, but their sea voyage was agonizing and long. To help pass time, Shek and Wong would fish by tying pieces of rags to their hooks and tossing the line over the ship's railing.

During the steel-cold nights, Shek made sure his little brother had enough hot tea and blankets to stay warm.

After almost two months on the stormy seas, they finally arrived in San Francisco. Like many others on board, Shek and Wong were frail from their exhausting trip. However, the brothers were excited.

"Look, Little Wong, this is the land of opportunity!" Shek exclaimed as he stared out at the new world.

Horses and wagons met them at the ship. Shek made sure he was close to his little brother as the Chinese were separated into groups heading for Sacramento. "Stay close," Shek whispered.

Chinese laborers had been hired by the Central Pacific Railroad Company to build railroad tracks headed east. Irish railroad workers had been hired by the Union Pacific Railroad Company, and starting from Omaha, Nebraska, they headed west. When the two railroad companies met in Utah, passengers and cargo would be able to cross the continent in days instead of months.

The bosses hired by Central Pacific did not believe the Chinese could endure the building of the railroad—on average they were skinny and looked upon as mere weaklings. The bosses made fun of their straw hats, pajama-like clothes and even their long queues, braids which they wore down the center of their backs.

"Coolies," they called the Chinese. Lowly workers.

The Chinese laborers began each day at dawn and continued until dusk. Side by side, Shek and Wong worked with heavy sledge-hammers that they slammed into the spikes till their blistered hands bled. The cart full of tools and supplies would trail up and down the rail line as the workers hammered under the beaming hot sun.

Day by day by day they labored through desert hills, through meadows, and across steep cliffs until they were met by rows of mountains, which the foreman called "the Sierras."

The loud whistle sounded each evening, a signal to the end of a hard workday. When the Chinese laborers returned to their camps, the cooks prepared hot water in tubs so the exhausted workers could bathe.

The brothers also looked forward to mealtime, when the cooks prepared their favorite Cantonese dishes—rice with dried fish, mushrooms, bamboo shoots, vegetables, pork, seaweed, salted cuttlefish, noodles, and, of course, hot tea.

Many nights Shek shared his own food with his little brother. "Make sure you finish every grain of rice for Ma," he would say.

The brothers slept in a tent so fragile, the harsh wind nearly blew it away, but inside the tent each night Shek cupped Little Wong's hand and helped his brother practice his Chinese calligraphy.

Once a month they wrote to their mother and sent money across the sea to her.

Ma, they wrote. *We hope you are able to buy some crops with this money. Please do not worry about us. Even in this foreign land, someday our family will be rich forever. Your sons, Shek and Wong.*

One hot afternoon, the brothers were still working to cross the Sierras when the boss pulled Little Wong aside. "You, Coolie, we have to blow up this side of the mountain to build a tunnel for the tracks. You're the smallest, get into the basket to set the dynamite."

With the little English he knew, Shek shouted, "He too young! I am small too. I set dynamite." He was afraid his little brother would lose his fingers or toes in the explosion.

The boss nodded. Lowered in the hand-made basket, Shek balanced himself against the harsh wind. He made sure the wick on the dynamite was long enough so the workers had plenty of time to pull him up away from the blast. Using a hand pick, he dug a small opening and placed the dynamite carefully into the hole. After Shek lighted the wick he shouted, *"Fie dee!"* Hurry up! Wong and the workers quickly pulled him away from the blast. On the ground, Shek sighed in relief.

As seasons passed, the Chinese laborers carried twice their expected workloads at astonishing speeds!

At the end of exhausting workdays, Shek and Wong were always glad to get back to their tent. One time, as they headed to their camp on the newly leveled earth, Shek turned to admire a trestle they had just finished. "Someday our family will see our great accomplishment," he said to his little brother.

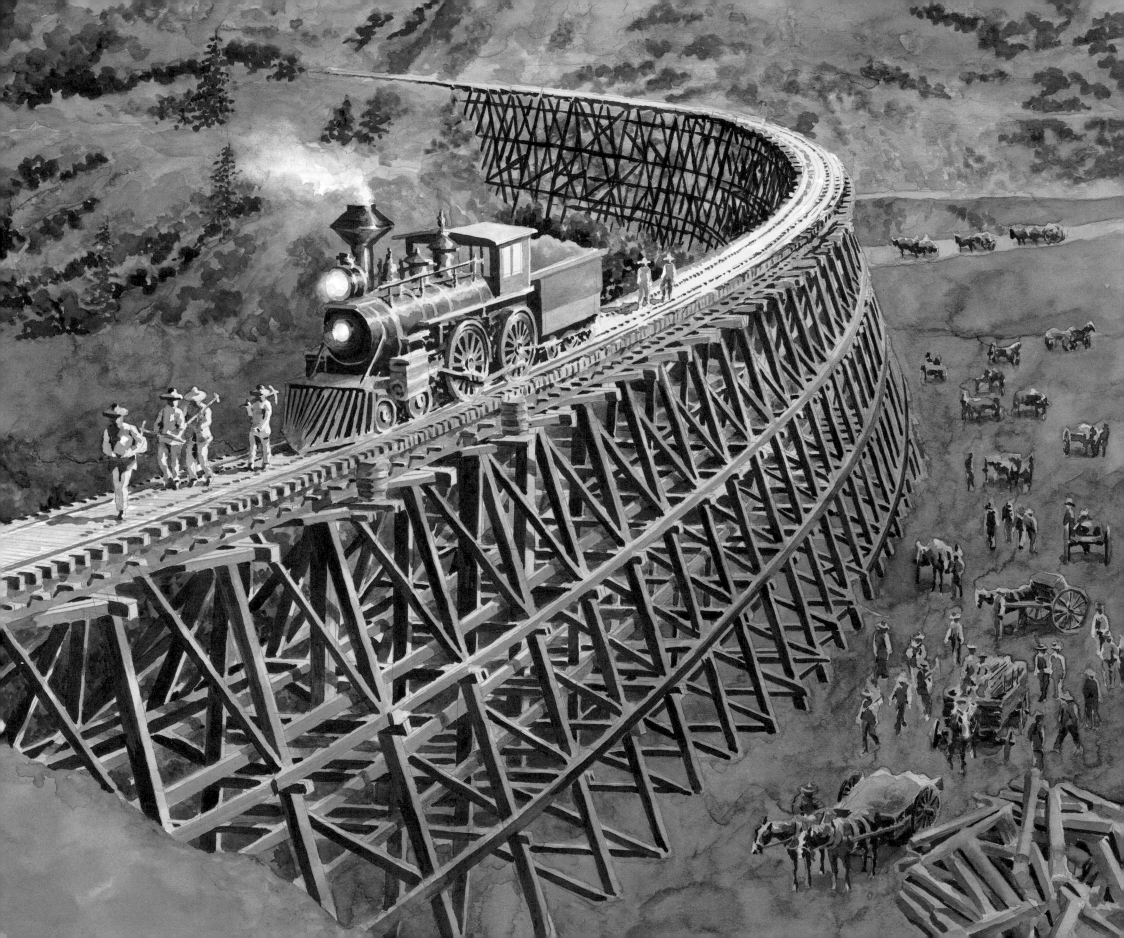

The Chinese worked in twelve-hour shifts. They pecked, drilled, and hacked through more and more mountains and hard rock face. Conditions grew dangerously worse. Then the Chinese workers discovered that other, non-Chinese laborers were paid more than they!

Were they discriminated against because of their long queues and almond-shaped eyes? The Chinese laborers thought so. They spoke little English and felt helpless.

Then, one June day, some three thousand graders, tunnelmen, and road pavers joined forces and stopped working. They chanted over and over in English, "Equal pay! Equal hours!"

The bosses were furious. "We're not going to tolerate this. No water and no food until you return to work. If you don't cooperate, we'll send you all back to China!"

The cooks sneaked barrels of hot tea for the protesters to survive during the cold nights. But with the lack of food and water, in days many of them grew weak. Many of them wondered if the protest should continue.

Finally, one night, the workers gathered. Many spoke, then Shek stood up. "We will all starve if we continue to strike. We must not forget why we came here." Nobody answered. Then, one by one, the workers nodded. They thought of their suffering families back home and agreed to return to work the next day.

That very night Shek wrote to reassure their mother. *Ma. Please do not worry. We have plenty to eat here in this land of opportunity. Our family will never go hungry again and soon we will have a feast together! Shek.*

The United States government pushed the railroad companies to complete the railroad project faster and faster. The two companies were paid by the number of miles. The bosses in turn demanded and pushed their workers to perform faster and faster.

Over the winter, the laborers raised trestles, shoveled the fills, and built mile after mile of snowsheds until they finally came down to the foothills in Nevada. There, a snowstorm raged across the countryside. With fear of an avalanche—one had swept away a crew of workers a year earlier—the laborers shoveled relentlessly through the blanket of snow.

As usual, Shek made sure his little brother was by his side.

Then, in the late afternoon, while the storm still raged, a roaring, crashing sound rolled down on them. Avalanche! Panicked, Wong peered through the windy snow. "Shek, where are you?" he shouted.

There was no sign of his older brother anywhere. Wong shouted in Chinese at the other workers, "My brother is buried in the snow! Please, please help find him! He'll freeze to death!"

The boss ran up from the rear and grabbed Wong's arm. "Back to work! You, Coolie, enough! Back to work!" Wong pulled himself free and began to dig frantically through the snow with his bare hands. He remembered his older brother's words that they would never be apart.

Finally Wong saw the tip of Shek's boot protruding above the alp of snow! "*Gow man!*" he shouted. Help!

He had found him.

The workers helped to dig Shek out of the snow. They found him half-frozen and clinging to his shovel, but alive.

Wong took off his brown smock and wrapped it around his older brother's frost-bitten body. A cook ran to him with a cup of hot tea as the workers carried Shek over to a bamboo mat in a nearby tent.

In his arms, Wong cradled Shek and massaged his older brother's shivering body until it began to feel warm. *"Yum cha,"* Wong said. Drink tea, my brother.

"I . . . will . . . get better . . . ," Shek muttered back. "I must."

As the days passed, Shek became better and better. Though he lost two toes from frostbite, he was soon back at his brother's side. Back at his sledgehammer, hammering the rails across the deserts and mountains and prairies of the western expanse.

Four years later—it was spring 1869—the Chinese laborers made their way to Promontory Summit, Utah. The two railway lines, Union Pacific and Central Pacific—built by the Irish workers from the East, and mostly Chinese workers from the West—would meet there. When they met, there was a big celebration. Railroad managers, towns-people, and other workers were invited, but not the Chinese, not the coolies.

Wong and Shek stood back and watched the ceremony from behind the crowd of reporters and cameras.

"We know," Shek said to Wong. "Call us what you will, it is our hands that helped build the railroad."

After the ceremony the brothers did not go back to China. Instead, they took the money they had saved and rode west on the new train to find a new home.

They settled in San Francisco. One day, gathering his thoughts, Wong took out his brush and ink block and started to write.

Ma. It has been quite some time since we last wrote. Shek is busy minding the store. Already the community in Chinatown knows me as the letter writer! Now I help those who can't read and write send letters home to their families in China. We are hopeful and excited that soon we shall be reunited with you and our brothers here in America, the land of opportunity. Wong.

Soon enough, the brothers sent money home again. However, this time it was money for their family to join them in America.

PawPaw starts a fire in the wastebasket and prepares the firecrackers in the backyard.

"Now are you ready to pay respect to our ancestors?" my grandmother calls out to me. "Take the paper money and gold paper and throw it in the flames. It will make your ancestors rich in the spirit world forever."

As I watch the ashes disappear into the sky, I know I will remember my ancestors. How could I forget?

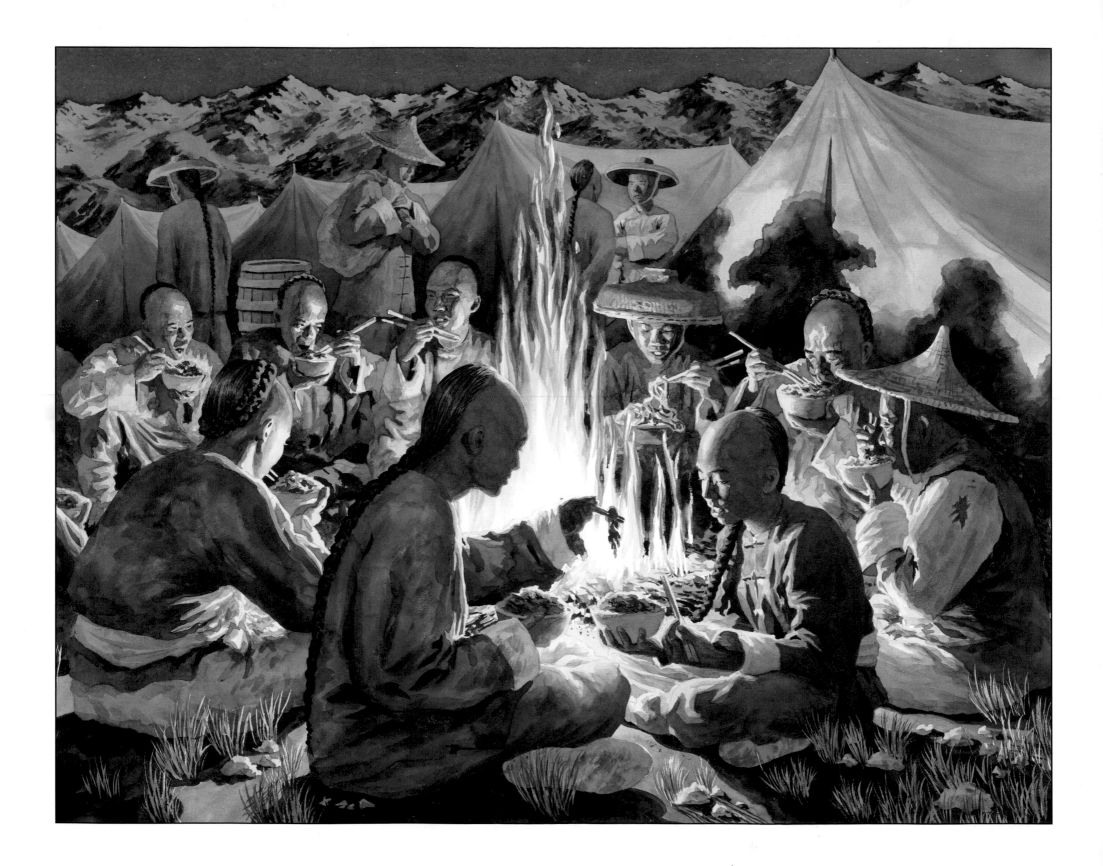

AUTHOR'S NOTE

The story was inspired by actual historical events in the history of the American railroad. Thousands of Chinese fled to America in the mid-1800s because of famine and the Taiping Rebellion, in which the people of China revolted against the imperial government that reigned at that time.

In researching the early Chinese Americans, I found their involvement with the transcontinental railroad fascinating. With primitive equipment and their ethics of hard work, these people, derisively called coolies, gave new meaning to the word. I wanted their brave story to be told in a way that would have the most impact, and so I chose to tell it through the personal experiences of two brothers.

The Chinese laborers endured the most brutal prejudice in their newly adopted land. They were looked upon as evil foreigners and hated by the early settlers. There is little question that they were given the more dangerous and lower-paying tasks. There were even riots against the Chinese working on the rails; many were beaten and some were killed.

Despite all the anti-Chinese attacks, snow and rock avalanches, fierce weather conditions, and blasting accidents, the Chinese laborers worked harder and harder. Their achievement—hammering a railroad out of hundreds of miles of treacherous and unexplored country—remains an incredible feat.

In the making of the railroad, thousands of Chinese lost their lives. Some of the recovered bodies were sent back to their families in China. Many were undiscovered and forgotten, and their graves remain unknown and scattered along the trackside, a silent tribute to their accomplishment.

The Ching Ming Festival, meaning *Supreme Light,* is the day for the dead, usually celebrated on the fourth or fifth of April (according to the lunar calendar). It is a day when Chinese families pay their respect to their ancestors, to people like Shek and Wong, who never forgot their family and became an important part of this new country they called "the land of opportunity."

to my mother for her strength and my father for his sacrifices —Y I N

with special appreciation to Patti Gauch and Cecilia Yung —C. K. S.

BIBLIOGRAPHY

Bain, David Haward. *Empire Express: Building the First Transcontinental Railroad.* New York: Viking, 1999.

Fraser, Mary Ann. *Ten Mile Day: And the Building of the Transcontinental Railroad.* New York: Henry Holt and Company, 1993.

Hoobler, Dorothy, and Thomas Hoobler. *The Chinese American Family Album.* New York: Oxford University Press, 1994.

McCunn, Ruthanne Lum. *An Illustrated History of the Chinese in America.* San Francisco: Design Enterprises of San Francisco, 1979.

Meltzer, Milton. *The Chinese Americans.* New York: Crowell, 1980.

Sinnott, Susan. *Chinese Railroad Workers.* Chicago: Franklin Watts, 1994.

Stein, R. Conrad. *The Transcontinental Railroad in American History.* Springfield, N.J.: Enslow Publishers, Inc., 1997.

Young, Robert. *The Transcontinental Railroad: America at its Best?* Parsippany, N.J.: Dillon Press, 1997.

PATRICIA LEE GAUCH, EDITOR

Text copyright © 2001 by Yin. Illustrations copyright © 2001 by Chris K. Soentpiet. All rights reserved. This book, or parts thereof, may not be reproduced in any form without permission in writing from the publisher, Philomel Books, a division of Penguin Putnam Books for Young Readers, 345 Hudson Street, New York, NY 10014. Philomel Books, Reg. U.S. Pat. & Tm. Off. Published simultaneously in Canada. Printed in Hong Kong by South China Printing Co. (1988) Ltd. Book design by Gunta Alexander. The text is set in Columbus.
The art was done in watercolors on watercolor paper.

Library of Congress Cataloging-in Publication Data   Yin. Coolies / by Yin ; illustrated by Chris K. Soentpiet.   p.   cm.
Summary: A young boy hears the story of his great-great-great-grandfather and his brother who came to the United States to make a better life for themselves helping to build the transcontinental railroad. 1. Chinese Americans—Juvenile fiction. [1. Chinese Americans—Fiction. 2. Brothers—Fiction. 3. Central Pacific Railroad Company—Fiction. 4. Railroads—Fiction.] I. Soentpiet, Chris K., ill. II. Title.   PZ7.S685273Co   2001   [E]—dc21   98-40403   CIP   AC
ISBN 0-399-23227-3 (hc : alk. paper)   10 9 8 7 6 5 4 3 2 1   First Impression